For The Muss
Sam Williams

For my lovely daughter Maja
Cecilia Johansson

First published in Great Britain in 2016 by Boxer Books Limited
www.boxerbooks.com
Boxer® is a registered trademark of Boxer Books Limited
Text copyright © 2016 Sam Williams
Illustrations copyright © 2016 Cecilia Johansson
The rights of Sam Williams and Cecilia Johansson to be identified as the author and illustrator
of this work have been asserted by them in accordance with
the Copyright, Designs and Patents Act, 1988.
All rights reserved, including the right of reproduction in whole or in part in any form.
A catalogue record of this book is available from the British Library.
The illustrations were prepared digitally.
The text is set in Adobe Garamond Pro
ISBN 978-1-910126-62-2
1 3 5 7 9 10 8 6 4 2
Printed in China
All of our papers are sourced from managed forests and renewable resources.

Croc?
What Croc?

Written by Sam Williams

Illustrated by Cecilia Johansson

Boxer Books

Little Fluff sauntered by
the river. He was on his way
to meet a friend for a picnic.

"Croc!" shouted Flamingo.
Little Fluff looked puzzled.

"Croc? What croc?"
said Little Fluff, skipping
over a rock and laughing.

"Croc!"

shouted Monkey.

Little Fluff looked around.

"Croc? What croc?"
asked Little Fluff,
flying through the air.

"Croc!"

shouted Elephant.

"Croc? What croc?" asked Little Fluff,
leaping over a big muddy hole.

"Gorilla!"

Little Fluff shouted.

"Crocodile!"
shouted Gorilla.

"Arghhhhhh,"
screamed Crocodile,
"Gorilla!"
and jumped into the river.

Gorilla scooped Little Fluff
up with his big, strong arms.
"Hello, Little Fluff. I didn't know
you were bringing a friend?"
"I wasn't," laughed Little Fluff.

So Little Fluff and Gorilla sat down on the riverbank and had the most wonderful picnic – just the two of them . . . without a croc in sight!